My Heart's Journey

My Heart's Journey

Nada Bazih

Dedication
This book is dedicated to my parents, who taught me so much about love and forgiveness.

My Heart's Journey

Table of Contents

Chapter One

Four Elements

It was not you, only your spirit following me around wherever I went. I never imagined something so invisible could have such a clear presence in my life. It touches me, resides in my senses, and draws within me all feelings of fear and desire at the same time. Then it leaves me, wondering if it ever visited me, or whether my experience was nothing but a dream.

How many things in life happen to us only to make us more confused, less certain of who we are, or what we are capable of becoming? It is no coincidence that I met you. Heaven had arranged for us such a meeting. There was always a purpose of love. One we understand only after we have lost, won, or achieved both equally. Is there ever victory in love? The biggest achievement is an interrupted dream we are able to complete on a pillow that never responded to reality.

There was a breeze coming from the graveyard behind me. It carried with it scents so familiar I could hardly ignore it. Now I was more confused. How could life and death belong to the same place at the same time? Little did I know that the deeper we hide our dreams, the less possible it is for them to vanish. They feed from the soil, only to become stronger and visit us with a different texture every time. I had intended to play a game with destiny. It was never meant as pride, only a way of showing me that love, being coincidence, was also a choice we can only wish to make.

Knowing you had made it easy for me to draw the shape of my heart at an early age. At least that is what you made me believe. I had major roles in the scripts you wrote. Yet, in that particular one, I was a heroine, one who did not know that her role was erasing her own heart. She held the imaginary brush and you made the moves. You moved in every direction this heroine might have desired. After that, you stood in the darkness and watched how your movements had turned the painting into a question mark. You uttered few words as you watched my tears merge into your moves.

"Passion, not patience, is what we need to be free." That was my first lesson. I wish I understood what you meant then. It would have saved me a journey so long, it almost made me believe in fortune telling; so hard it transformed my heart into particles, ready to be washed away any time by imaginary waves of love.

I resumed the walk and carried my stitched veins with me. They were once cut off so I could feel you no more. As if our veins had addiction edges we are able to cut off at any time. You were not my addiction. You were the nerve causing all other addictions. It was a very unusual transformation, one I never imagined for myself, not even in my childhood dreams.

I put on that white dress you once gave me, and I decided to take a long walk and visit each graveyard that came my way. Perhaps I could recognize a hand waving to be saved from dying too soon. There could be buried lovers who long to be saved and resume a journey so incomplete. Just as I approached the last graveyard, I heard a cry. I recognized the voice. I had known him a long time ago. He was not a lover, only a soul mate. He loved another woman. He and I were soul mates, not lovers. She had left him for someone else. It was not a choice. The man she had left him for had saved her from drowning one day. Since then, he had become her source of living. She could only breathe when he was around her. Remembering the cycle of life and the importance of oxygen particles in a human's life, I wondered if you were able to survive all those years? "We do not need breathing to be alive. Love is what makes our cycle go round." This is what you told me one day. And I believed you with all the innocence that a child could have, when promised the escape from the highest waves of nature. And I am glad I did believe you then.

You were the wildest ocean I had ever visited, always unpredictable. Your waves were never on time. They always blew me away when I expected them the least. Yet they worshipped me quietly after I had walked away.

An Algerian writer once said that love is most beautiful when we find it while looking for something else. I do not remember looking for anything when I found you. Or maybe I was looking for everything a child could hope for after death separated her from her twin sister, a twin sister who was only seven seconds younger. Seconds are too long of a time for people to fall in love.

In a lover's world time may not exist. Love is a thunderstorm that happens on a sunny day. You cannot really tell how suddenly it happens, but you feel it so strongly it threatens your own existence. What would a girl who had just lost her twin sister be looking for, friendship, another sister, or maybe a cure? A cure: that is what a young heart needs after it has been ripped apart, thrown into destiny, and left to rotate between heaven and hell.

She was my sister and my best friend. We were sisters who looked the same, and friends whose differences only drew us closer. She was the younger and wiser one.

Before going to sleep each night, she and I would lie down, side by side, exchanging endless talks of who we might become one day. She wanted to be a mother. That was a fantasy she was too young to achieve. Death chose her instead.

How can we be too young for something we know by instinct, yet too ready for something we do not even wish to know? Perhaps that is where the perplexity of existence lies and tried to confirm itself by twisting our destinies into a toy which death decided to play with any time it decided the time is right. It did not even ask us if we had completed our earthly missions or not.

They say sadness diminishes as time goes by. The sadness I felt after losing my sister seemed to grow stronger each day. I was alone for the first time. Despite having many people around me, I decided to confirm my loneliness by spending time with myself, away from those who walked at the surface of my heart, without stepping once accidentally inside.

In my loneliness I found peace. There was no show to run, or a role to play. There was one scene with a single actress and only one person watching. One scene was enough to determine the rest of my life. It was my first year of college. I had taken an acting class with an attempt to overcome my loneliness in a different way. I had to do that, since sharing life's smallest details with my sister was no longer possible. I thought maybe interacting with other characters would help me establish new relationships, imaginary ones perhaps.

What I did not know was that from the first cast meeting I was chosen to play the role alone. All the other characters were part of the setting. We were not supposed to interact with one another. How would people understand my loneliness after that?

The rules were so strict about us not interacting with one another. The director wanted to experiment with something. He wanted to see if harmony would exist if characters did not know one another. How brilliant I thought he was after my own theatrical experience transformed me into a woman capable of directing her own destiny, or so I thought. "I heard you are mourning the death of a loved one." A voice from behind me spoke softly into my ear.

In three seconds, I turned back and gazed into the eyes that froze time within me and everywhere around me eternally. I do not know what I became or on what planet I had landed. I could hear or see no one around me, not even to whom those eyes belonged. There was no need, not even for that. Two jewels simplified all that I needed to know about my current being. They carried inside them life's most precious elements: earth, water, fire and air. They were solid like the soil, so determined in what they desired. They were two burning torches that unintentionally heated all that was around them, only to become stronger, more capable of heat.

Just like the wildest sea that keeps changing colors to suit its mood, those two torches swung up and down, each time with a different movement that altered between heaven and earth. They were called the torches of life, because the air element inside them gave them the power to set life into the spirits they approached.

And this time I was the object. Only if I could go back to earth. In three seconds, I had become a woman with no dimensions. I knew exactly where I belonged, but I was too paralyzed to get there. If only I could have borrowed a flame from those eyes and run away, escaped into the nearest iceberg. There it would have been impossible for them to burn me. I would have stayed until I became ice. Then they would recognize me from my breathlessness, which I would no longer be able to regulate.

As if he sensed my feelings. He interrupted me saying, "I have been thinking about your sorrow. Each day I get more confused." "How so?" I asked.

"Unlike other people, your pain seems to grow stronger each day since the incident," he said.

"Perhaps I have not found a cure yet," he continued.

"I am a doctor of alternative medicine. No chemicals are included in my treatment. It is all natural," he said.

Suddenly the curtain opened. I took center stage to proceed with my role, and he positioned himself right behind me, so that the scene would go on. Who was this man? Three seconds were not enough for all my questions to be answered, but they were the exact moments needed for my heart to enter a battlefield of excitement.

I heard someone once say that love is a battlefield. We approach it with a desire to conquer the person's heart, only to discover that we should have been more prepared, with more weapons and less expectations. During the performance I was talking to the audience, and he was talking to me. No one could hear him but me. Perhaps he was not talking. What was this voice, repeating the words over and over again? "I am a doctor of alternative medicine."

It could have been my imagination celebrating for finally finding some cure. In the little town where I live, I had heard of seven doctors of alternative medicine who claimed to heal people. One of the doctors had visited our house when a friend who was staying with us suddenly had a severe headache. My brother was able to get hold of the doctor. I led him into the room where my friend was lying down, unable to take a glance at the man who came to help her.

"Bring me a bowl of apple cider vinegar and a piece of cloth," he said.

So I did, and silently watched his hands place the vinegar soaked cloth on my friend's forehead. He massaged her head softly.

"Let it sit there for half an hour," he added. Then he left the room. I stayed watching my friend to see how in less than an hour her pain gradually subsided. She was finally able to open her eyes and take a glance at what was around her. I have always believed in alternative medicine. The reasons are as simple as the man's words: no chemicals added or involved.

My grandmother had told me one day that God has a cure to each and every illness. The cures are all around us, in the simplest ways possible: herbs, naturally grown foods and honey to name a few. And now vinegar has proven to be another good example. The reason I believed what my grandmother said is because no single remedy she suggested ever proved to be ineffective.

My grandmother lived for over a hundred years. She was around during the different stages of my life, from the years of childhood curiosity to those of disappointing adulthood. I had endless talks with her days and nights about life, the after and those few things in between. She had so much wisdom. In her town she was the only woman who socialized with men on regular basis despite the traditions that prohibited socializing, not to flirt with them, but to bring more connections to my grandfather. The older she grew, the more capable she became of spreading her wisdom to those who needed it. Approaching her hundredth birthday did not stop her from gathering the whole family around her to listen to her legendary stories.

I cannot count the times I laid down next to her, listening to her words that caused my imagination to travel around the world and meet with unusual people and experience unusual incidents. It now strikes me that I never had the chance to ask her about the subject that puzzled me the most, love. In all her stories, love was a theme. I listened and enjoyed it only. I did not wonder about the difficult side of love while listening to my grandmother. When the story was about a woman who loved a man and decided to marry another, all that I could conclude was that it was an unhappy ending. I never asked my grandmother why love gets that way sometimes. I never asked her whether we can love someone and marry another, or what it would take for love to always have a happy ending.

My grandmother died at the age of one hundred and six and some of her answers were buried with her. If only she had lived a few more years to solve my riddles.

Life sometimes works in a funny way. How many times do we wonder about things, and just when the moment is right for us to ask a question, do we realize that forgetfulness suddenly takes over? Perhaps our most puzzling questions were not meant to be answered. Maybe it is our destiny to experience those answers for ourselves to become our own masters; independent from those many things that distract our being.

The last magical experience I myself had lived was that of the three seconds that fashioned and shaped the rest of my life. After that, experiences started to exist with no time or place. The only proof of my being was the feeling residing in my veins after each event.

Because time and place were love's worst enemies, I decided to forget about the three seconds, the stage and the thought of the man who claimed to have a cure for a heart he never knew before. I did not want anything to have so much control over me. Sadness after losing my sister had already had its share of my heart.

Chapter Two

What Is Love?

Destiny throws at us a few decisions to make us believe that we are the leaders in our lives. It stands aside and watches how this, belied to the sane person, diminishes every day. Just like the rain that suddenly hits a sunny day, or a wind so strong it reshapes that part of nature, so do the incidents of love attack a man's heart without warning.

Just when I thought I would never see those captivating eyes again, I noticed them watching me from far away. I do not remember when or where that happened. I had completely lost touch with time, dimension or anything tangible. Once again everything around me stopped. I could see or hear nothing. I entered into the eyes that had promised me a cure, so natural it was made from their own essence.

I cannot remember how long I stayed there before your carriage of words was waiting to drive me back to reality.

"I am glad to see you recovering. You must be taking the medicine I gave you. There is an end to everything. Even sorrow deserts our hearts after we torture it with endless nights of crying and sadness." he said.

"And the medicine?" he added.

"I try not to depend on it," I said.

"It contains no chemicals," he replied.

"And so they say about love," I said. It was funny I had mentioned the word love. I had been familiar with it only the day I locked eyes with this man. How could I know so much about it? It invaded every aspect of my soul that I could no longer be an outsider. It was my companion, my friend and my enemy all at once. Yes! It was my enemy every time this man was not around; every time his spirit was not surrounding me.

"Let us take a walk," he said.

I did not utter a word. All that I cared about was to be with him in a moment measured by no time; in a place that only imagination could remember. There we stood, in his paradise, trying to remember if we had known each other in previous lives, or if perhaps our souls were matched in heaven only to belong to two different beings here on earth. The feeling was so familiar it made me forget that I had not even asked him about his name or about any other thing that belonged to him. Could this be better? Why did I need to know his name, age, or what he does? All those things belonged to ordinary stories. And something about our meetings told me that our story would not be ordinary.

"It does not matter which medicine you take first," he said.

He had given me three tubes with pills inside. They were of identical color and size. The only way I would recognize them was by their taste. The first one was so bitter that I had to take it first. The second one tasted as delicious as the taste of life could get sometimes. And the third one had no taste at all. It made me lose hope in healing every time I swallowed it.

What did he mean by all that? He was the doctor, so he definitely knew what he was doing. This is what I had always thought to myself. It did not matter if I got healed anymore. All that mattered was that I saw him; became a part of his life, his destiny and maybe his dreams.

He was not always around. That left me puzzled. The feeling possessed me. I could feel, smell and taste his spirit, yet he was not there.

What is love? I kept asking myself that question every time this man was not around. Was it missing someone till you lost the logic of thinking? How could I call it love after that? Was love something we were aware of? Or was it that power that takes control over your being until it threatens your own existence? This was what had been happening to me. I had a new illness. Was it him having power over me? Or could it have been the medicine he gave me? Or did it really matter at that point?

"I have been driving all night to see your beautiful face," he said.

Was this voice talking to me? Or was that an angel uttering peaceful words for Mother Nature to relax? No! It was him. I recognized him from the golden hair that reminded me of barley fields I once walked on. I recognized him from the smile that shone and the eyes that held the innocence of a child. How could this have been possible?

This man almost poisoned me with love, yet he made me want to cry every time I saw his face.

"I have been missing you," I replied. I do not know where I got the courage to say those words. The truth was that when I was with him, I forgot about all the customs and traditions that I had been taught. His words became the rules that I accepted to follow. And without his rules I had no sense of direction. I forgot where I came from or where I was going. He held my hand and kissed it gently. I do not know what I became then. I found myself to be a child all over again, meeting with her first love.

I could have been everything. But one thing I could not do was look him in the eye and tell him what that little touch of his lips on my hand did to me. It was nighttime. It was a rainy night with a very cold breeze. He asked me if I would like a cup of herbal tea. I accepted it without thinking. Men usually ask you to drink coffee. But everything about this man was different. He was an herbalist after all. And he knew that I had a taste for what is unique in life.

Was he like that too? I thought.

"Who are you?" I asked him calmly.

"I am a humbled soul," he gently replied.

"Are you truly an herbalist?" I asked.

"I am," he said.

"Could you please explain?" I asked.

"I was born in a small town and because of that I felt that I belonged to the whole world and needed to heal the world," he said.

"The whole world, huh?" I said.

He smiled. "And your heart?" I asked.

"Inseparable from my body. What about it?" he said.

"Has it settled in a place yet?" I asked.

He remained silent and gazed into my eyes for a long time but said nothing. His looks make my soul fly. They took it to strange places, places it had never visited before. The places seemed like fairy tale places. I wondered why this was happening to me. Was it the pills again? Or was it him?

Who was this man? Where was he born and why did destiny choose me to have such an encounter with him? I guess that is why they call it destiny. We have so little control over whom we meet, love and marry. And if destiny had nothing to do with it, then what did? This man did not look like any other I had met before. He did not speak the language of men. And he was not available as much as most people are. He came and went just like the forces of nature. They have so much impact and cause so much damage, yet we can never stop them. They determine our destiny. And with all the sorrow that they create, there is something so essential about them. They complete the cycle of humanity and creation.

He was either a test or a kind of punishment. Yes! This man was a test for me. Who had I become after meeting this man? Was I still that innocent girl who waited for nothing but a simple relation of true love with a man who was as clear as the sun? Perhaps not anymore, not after I had looked at him, smiled and even kissed his eyes. They were so beautiful. He kept them closed for a very long time after I did that, and when he finally opened them, he told me that he had been meditating. He was so happy. And I was happy, because I had touched the ocean. I felt like a mermaid, because he was the ocean. And no reality could change that.

How naïve I can be sometimes. I was younger than a child who dreamed about true love. What could happen to a child who's trying to defy the ocean waves? Who would mess with the ocean? It is the wildest creature God ever created. And yet I did not care.

Why would I care? In most of the stories that I had heard about or read; the ending was happy. For this I decided to take big steps. And sometimes I even jumped. I am not sure if he ever noticed. But he did seem startled and amazed with what I did. He quite understood the child inside of me, yet he always treated me like a woman. He transformed me into someone I had never imagined to be. It was a quick process. It did not give me the chance to question whether it was a good or a bad transformation. I wanted to grow up. And I wanted to do that only through him. I placed my family and friends aside for a while. The only part they played in the huge play was watching me change every day. They were not sure of the reason. They thought maybe my sister's death influenced me dearly. And that was true. It sure did. It made me feel empty and incomplete, as if part of me was always missing. I missed her every day. And because of that my love for this man grew only stronger. He was not only the herbalist who was helping me heal, but also the man who was raising me up;

preparing me for that huge mystery we call life. He prepared me for almost anything except having the strength to live one single day without him.

Days passed by without me seeing him or hearing his voice. For so many nights and days I wondered about what he might be doing or with whom he might be spending his time. I had never even asked him his name. I never asked him about anything that might reveal his identity. Why did I do that? I am not sure. That reminded me of those few things that happen to us in life only to confuse us and to make us unaware of who we are or whom we can become. Perhaps he intentionally kept himself a mystery, to give me something to think about.

He had told me once that he was my future. I wondered what he meant by that. He knew what he was talking about. But I did not. How could I know anything beyond what he told me? I took all of his words for granted. They were the only truth that I wanted to know. I looked into his eyes and learned all that he needed to teach me. That was the best school experience I have ever had. There was no difficulty in memorizing things. Looking into his eyes was the process for information to be carved in my memory forever. During this experience I never wanted time to end, but it did. And it did fast, because he was the one who decided when the classes began and when they ended. He only had to sigh for me to understand that he needed a break.

Chapter 3

My Heart's Journey

I have not been into my soul for so many days, even more than that; much more than time can ever trace. I have almost forgotten about the herbalist, my twin sister and even loss itself. I was sleeping perhaps. It was a long nap, so deep I entered the world of angels, genies and undefined species. It was so serene, so different from worldly experiences.

There is no proper language to describe it. It was with other people; some I knew, some I did not know, yet I was alone. It was my own dream, my own experience. Others were in it, but it was happening to me. I am alone for the first time, but I am neither lonely nor scared.

I cannot remember much more of the dream. But I do know that after waking up I had this indescribable thirst for life. I was hungry for love; for all the experiences that I have been depriving myself from for so long. I wanted to breathe, swim, go to school, cook and hug the world. I needed for the first time to be the choreographer of my own life.

There is so much dust on the window inside my bedroom. I do not feel like wiping it. I want to open the window and watch the rain wash the window clean. My phone did not ring while I was sleeping, otherwise I would have awakened. I am starting to wonder what might have happened to everyone when I suddenly realize that the nap was only for half an hour. My hands are still numb. I must have been exhausted. I sit down for a while and take a look at all that's around me. It seems I have been away from this place for a very long time. I check the closet. My clothes are still there. I look at the perfume bottle. It's still full. Through the window I see my neighbor's red curtain. Children are playing inside my neighbor's yard. I cheer. Nothing has really changed except my awakening after a short nap. I will wait till the numbness goes away. Then I will check all the other rooms, the attic and the backyard.

There are no tasks for me to do. My hair is a little wet. And the towel is still hanging on my chair, next to mom and dad's picture. They are beautiful together. I need to call them and ask them how long I have been away. They could be worried.

I am in the kitchen, making a honey sandwich. The jar is almost empty. I add some dried cranberries to the sandwich. I move around the house very carefully so I can read the clues or try to understand for how long I have slept.

People do not change in thirty minutes. Something about time makes me move around the house faster, as if I have lost something. I move around the rooms, go up and down the stairs more than once.

A vase with purple flowers is sitting on my dining table. There are seven flowers inside the vase. They look so fresh, as if they have just been picked by the hands of a real gardener. I go back to the kitchen and make another sandwich. Writing is hanging on my fridge. It reads: "Behold, God is my helper. The Lord sustains my life." Mary had given me that. She is an angel. She would not believe in something less holy, less promising.

Mary and I were always close, but I have not seen her since our school days. Pictures of Mary and I are in the attic. I will go there. Maybe I can remember something.

There is a dim light coming from the attic. I follow it without hesitation.

I am a woman who has lost something a long time ago. I have been looking for it for a very long time. The nap was only a way for my soul to rest, to realize the dream of tomorrow, with all its good and bad. I follow the light carefully, yet fearlessly, with so much enthusiasm. It is a very comforting light. It reminds me of the church light at one of the AA meetings I attended with a friend. There was nothing in the attic but an open window and light from outside reflecting a picture of oregano leaves sprinkled over a loaf of bread on a coffee table somewhere in time. The back of a woman with dark hair is also in the picture. She seems indifferent to the meal in front of her. She is looking in a different direction. Her body is so determined in what she is seeing.

She could be waiting on her love. That reminds me of my beloved whom I have not seen in a long time. It is about time I moved in a different direction. I want to travel, search for the lost piece of my soul. Where is it hiding? I know it resides in a land somewhere, a near or far away land. It does not matter. All I know is that my heart is speaking to me. And I can never let my heart down. Our hearts speak truth to us. Sometimes we choose to ignore that.

I see faces old and new, black and white. But I recognize none. They are staring at me. Perhaps they know that I have disregarded my heart for a while. They want me to go ahead and look for you. It is a small world after all. But I do not see it that way. I have many thoughts racing in my head. I currently feel red, violet and blue. I am everything and nothing at the same time. My dreams had once been shattered. I am afraid to follow my heart steps this time. Where would I land? Whom would I meet? What would become of me? These are mysterious questions that only destiny can answer. It may also refuse to answer them.

I have to take the journey myself and see what will become of me. It is only fair and beautiful. A journey of love is what my heart is requesting of me. It has not felt love in a long time. It is longing for the connection that would make it alive again. This is only fair. And I have no way of saying no. My heart is dear to me. It has never asked me for anything before. How can I say no to the thing that introduced me to all the good things in life? My heart is not just an organ residing in my body. It is where my soul originated. And now it is asking me to take it on a trip, on a quest for life and love.

I am starting to get excited about all this. I am capable and together we can do it. I would not be alone. The passion inside both of us will light the way. No matter what the consequences, I am not alone. I have a purpose. I do not have many expectations; I have decided to enjoy the trip and make friends with nature.

I see the birds flying in groups. I see trees bending to kiss the ground. Perhaps they want to express their love for the earth. I see animals running around, trying to find the purpose of their own existence. They too have a purpose to be alive. They could be here for more than one purpose. They can be friends to man and to other animals. They enjoy nature like they've known her all their lives. And I enjoy this scene of harmony. I see flowers of different colors and shapes. These too have their purpose. They are here to decorate life, to remind us of the colors of each day. With the difficulties that each day may have, it still has a color and taste of its own.

Purple remains my favorite color when it comes to flowers and many other things. My beloved's spirit must be purple. It is unusual. This is what confuses me and makes me enthusiastic to go out looking for him. I want to see him again, ask him about all my wonders, the questions that only he could answer. The answers that would fill the great emptiness that was made the day we parted. It will not happen suddenly. It is going to be time for the emptiness to go away. Our departure was not smooth. It was so unexpected.

Some of my beliefs have changed since that departure. But I

still believe in true love. I would be scared to ever lose this belief. It gives me strength. It keeps me going in times of despair. So many things that happen around me could make me lose faith, but I decide to keep it. The fact that you are no longer here makes me go deeper into the meaning of love. And I do not wish to stop. I want to learn what love is all about. I want to write books about it and tell the whole world what I have learned. I want to experience it. Experiencing a thing is more powerful than just reading about it. I want to know about the miraculous power in changing people. Yet I do not want to experience it with just anyone. It has to be you or no one else. I am not sure why. You hold some kind of power over me. Maybe it is because you helped me heal. Or is it because you are not always available? I think it is because of all the truth you taught me about life.

My heart is with me on this journey, yet it remains so silent. I am scared. I speak to it and it does not answer the first time, or the second time. Then suddenly it speaks calmly and says: "True love requires patience." These few words make the blood inside my veins move upside down. They give me so much hope. I feel so alive. It makes so much sense what my heart just said. How beautiful! My heart knows what I needed to hear. That gives me hope. My journey is going to be long, and perhaps no one else is on this road except my heart and me. I must handle it with care.

Why have so many people given up? Why is there so much silence? Why do people choose to give up on love so fast? Do they not know that anything worth achieving requires time and effort to be achieved? It requires patience too. That is what my heart just said. Maybe these people did not know any better. Perhaps no one told them about love. I do not wish to blame them, for I do not know them. But I do wish my heart and I had more companions on the way. Someone could have sung, told a story or played a musical instrument. I do not anticipate success in this, but my heart gives me hope. And patience is usually rewarded.

How many people have walked this path before me? Where did they end up? Have they succeeded? I wonder about the obstacles waiting for me along this path. I am innocent of the charges. I did not choose love. It was love that hit me like a lightning strike on a sunny day. It took me by total surprise. And I did not resist, because there was pleasure in welcoming it. Love is a stranger that becomes close in a very short period of time. It became my family and my friends. Sweet is the love that comes unexpectedly. It teaches us about the miracle of life and the things that happen in it that make our beliefs change. Those beliefs, perhaps, needed to be changed, but the right force was not available for them to do so. Love does to us that which we cannot do to ourselves.

I feel pain. There are memories crossing my mind of people I left behind. I have gone too far. What would happen to Father and Mother? Despite leading a healthy life, dad is sick. I am worried about him. But I have to do this.

Father is a man of love himself. He struggled throughout his life to bring comfort to those around him. And so did Mother. They were a happy couple. I thank God for them. After I come back, I will explain to them what happened. They will understand. They are my family, and they know me so well.

During times of war Mom and Dad worried about us a lot. It was a silly war that took place when I was a child. It was a meaningless war. Is there ever a war with a cause? War destroys nations, countries, relations and so on. Is there ever a good outcome of it? Not that I have ever heard of.

Children are the ones who suffer the most during wars. It

shuts off their dreams, kills their hopes. I want to stop thinking about the war. I want to dream of something bright, perhaps of backyard weddings. Dreaming takes me faster to you. I want to place my head on your shoulder and cry. I want you to tell me the reasons you were away. And I pray your reasons are due to a cause. I know you will tell me the truth. You have never lied to me.

Chapter 4

On The Road

It is a rainy and chilly day. The path seems long. All I want to do is persevere. I want to know what is ahead. The road usually hides so many surprises. I love journeys, especially those with meaning. I want to see you and see what has become of you. Are you alive? Are you alone? Are you engaged with issues that are keeping you away from the world? I have shut myself away from worldly matters. I have chosen the spiritual path instead. I want to learn what it is like to be human. For this I connect with other beings and learn. I ask questions. I explore the depth of a human's soul and try to analyze it. Through this I have come to several conclusions.

One is that we have come here for a purpose, or perhaps we have come here for several purposes. Some of them are clear, others are hidden. We have come here to make a difference, to save or change a life.

Love is what connects us with other beings. And it does that so peacefully. It inspires us to dig for more meaning or create one. I have created a purpose since the day I last saw you. My purpose is to find you again, to see where the waves of life have taken you. This is important, not only because we love one another, but because we are human.

I walk silently this time. I think about nothing, and I speak no words. I let the path of love carry me in the direction it desires. I pass by couples on the road. Some couples are happy, others are not. There are those who pretend to be happy. How sad it is having to feign happiness. It takes a lot of hard work. The happy couples make me smile. Their image is beautiful. They gaze into each other's eyes like it is the first or last time they see each other. They smile like the whole world belongs to them. They cry tears of joy that cleanses the sadness that fills mother earth. They bring a cloud of hope into this world. I believe in them, and I see them as a good omen. They give me hope that you and I shall meet again. You and I, my love, have a meeting arranged in heaven that needs to be realized here on earth. I know you are waiting too. Your heart beats somewhere on this earth. All I have to do is listen carefully and follow the beats step by step until we finally collide. Our longing for one another is what would make us collide again.

I am worried that you might have lost your way. It is not easy having a purple spirit in a gray world.

I continue the path of love, not wanting to be recognized. What if I fail? What if I do not cross paths with you? I was created to dance with you, chase the birds together and love the morning together in silence. I see two love birds on my way. They resemble us. They seem to respect each other. Even birds understand the language of respect. You and I have spoken about the importance of that before. And you promised me that we will have respect for each other as long as we live.

I am missing my mother. Shouldn't she be with me on this path of unknown steps? Her words would help me persevere. I get encouraged every time I remember her words on love. Mother believes that true love is scarce but does exist. I believe her because she and my dad have a strong bond. With her simple words, she makes love seem so powerful.

This encourages me to go on with my journey. I am not sure what I am going to find. But I do know that the journey is worth taking.

I am not alone. My heart is my companion. It entertains me along the way. It sings to me songs of love. It cheers me up by questions that puzzled me. I am not sure if I am following its steps, or if it is following mine. There were times when it skips beats and I must catch up with it. And there are times when I decide to slow down. It waits for me. Amazing is the relationship that a man can have with his heart. It is so pure, so true. The two of us have become inseparable. It teaches me lessons throughout this journey. I have to walk the same steps it is taking. They are not ordinary steps. My heart seemed to know where it was going. It is determined, confident and not scared. I love that about my heart. Where did my heart learn all this? Did it belong to another body before belonging to me? How could that be possible?

I see that night is on the way. It is so quiet, so serene. I wish to ask it what it hides, but I am shy. What could it be hiding but lovers who do not wish to be seen?

Sometimes I wish to hide too. I am not sure why. Should I ask the night why? Is there danger in hiding? Why do lovers hide? Is this what my beloved does? I do not believe so. Destiny plays a part in what happens to us. I do not wish to ask destiny any questions. It could be holding a surprise for me, and I do not wish to spoil that. Things need to be unfolded at the right time. I shall wait, and so shall my heart.

We walk patiently towards our destiny. There is so much to see along the road, so much to wonder about. The owls decide to stay awake at night. What pleasure do they experience in this? There are many things which we may never know the answers to, but it is good to wonder about them. That is what makes life so amazing. The gap that is never filled is what makes some of us always startled, unwilling to rest. With the little knowledge I have about life it still fascinates me. And the thing that fascinates me the most is the absence of the man I love. How strange it is losing a first love!

I am sure there is a purpose in this. Our story makes me wonder about many things. Why did we not spend more time together? Why did I love you despite the mystery that surrounds you? And why did you love me despite my simplicity?

The road has become so quiet now that my questions have become silent. I want to stop asking questions for a short while and see what will unfold. I will give my heart a break, and I will take a break too. I am going to take a nap under the almond tree.

There is a dream I have. It is not a usual dream. In it I see all my loved ones. There is a birthday. I do not know to whom it belongs to. The dream is as incoherent as my thoughts are. I leave the birthday and wait for you outside. My friend passes by, inviting me to go swimming. I hesitate. I refuse to go. But I tell her that I am waiting for you. Lovers pass by. They are holding hands and dancing to the birthday music. Strangers pass by. They are indifferent to me. I now see you coming from far away. You are alone. You approach me and kiss my forehead. In the dream, just like in real life, I long for your answers. While you kiss my forehead, you whisper in my ear and say: "I am waiting for you to save me." "Save you from what." I say.

But you do not answer. Instead, you hold me close to you and stand in silence for a long time. All that is around us disappears. I no longer see lovers. I forget about the birthday or to whom it belongs. I forget about the gift or to whom I should have given it. We stand there in silence, lost in each other, waiting for the sky to glorify our union. And suddenly I am all alone. You are no longer there. I try to make sense of what has just happened when suddenly I hear the birthday song. I follow the sound and enter a room where I see all my loved ones dressed in white. I stand in the middle and start to cry.

My heart wakes me up from the dream with unusual heart beats. But I am still crying. How could I have had you with me a few minutes ago, and now it is only my heart I see? I cry, and my heart wipes my tears away. I do not know what to say. I wish our embrace was for a longer time. I wish I did not have to wake up so soon. My tears no longer make sense. I have to move on or move back. My heart wants me to move on. My heart is right. I have made a promise to myself to persevere. And I should keep my promise.

I hear Christmas music coming from far away. I almost lost touch with time. It must be Christmas now. The weather feels like it and so does the lovers' spirits. If it is Christmas, how come I am here? Where are my friends? I must have forgotten to wrap up the gifts. There are hearts that need to be warmed up. People need love more than they need gifts.

I am awaiting salvation. I am somewhere in the middle, scared to move forward, hesitant to go back. I must gain my strength back. I have a destination to reach.

I see a light from far away. A narrow road leads to it. I stare at it for a long time and wonder what it might be. I am curious. My curiosity grows, now that my heart beats faster. The light makes me nostalgic for places I have visited before. It reminds me of the light I followed at home. Should I follow the light this time? Where would it take me? I have to make my own decisions. I am responsible for myself. I am responsible for my heart too. Or is it the one responsible for me?

The light I see grows brighter sometimes. It increases my enthusiasm when this happens. I must figure out what is there. I am heading towards my destiny, and this place happens to be one of my stops. I can no longer wait. I consult with my heart, and my heart approves right away. We are both tired of being lonely. We want to move forward. We are both excited, wondering what could be waiting ahead for us. We move without hesitation. The road is narrow and lit only by the light that comes from far away. It is a long road, but our faith remains strong. We walk side by side, getting more enthusiastic with each step. My heart asks me several questions for which I have no answers. Perhaps I am not focused enough. I am already imagining what the source of the light could be. Could it be a movie theater or a night club?

My heart repeats the questions which I am trying to ignore. This time it is more determined to get answers. "Do you still love him?" my heart asks. This question leaves me breathless. I thought my heart had forgotten all about my love life. How could it forget? It is my heart after all. "Yes! I do still love him," I reply without hesitation. "Do you expect to see him again?" it asks. "I am not sure, but I want to," I reply. My heart remains quiet for a while, as if it is preparing for the next question. Then it asks me the question that has been puzzling me for a long time. "And where do you imagine he might be right now?" it asks. Before I have the time to think about the question, my tears start to fall. "I have no answer to that. All I care to know is that he is safe and happy," I say. "Is there a way to know that?" I ask my heart. But my heart remains silent, proceeds with the walk and asks no more questions.

Side by side we walk. This time I try to use my imagination and wonder about the lights I see from far away. What would I like them to be? I imagine all kinds of things. Children come to my mind first. Perhaps it is a childcare facility. Or it could be a place of worship. I will keep guessing until we get there.

My heart is unusually quiet. I do not know why. I intend to remain silent myself and not disturb it with more questions. My heart may already be exhausted from the journey.

We are getting closer to our destination. I pray this light brings new hope with it. I hope it has room for us to rest.

We are here. I can hardly believe it. What is this place? My heart and I remain silent. We do not wish to disturb anyone. It looks old. We walk towards the light. It leads us to a back room. We see an old man there. He is doing office work. We greet him and he greets us back.

"Excuse me. What is this place?" I ask.

"This is a military hospital," He replies.

I am not sure what to feel or say at this point. Is this good or bad? I do not ask my heart. I have exhausted it enough.

The old man asks where we have come from.

"I have come from far away. I do not remember for how long I have been gone or where exactly I came from. All I know is that I am here now, and I do need to rest. Would you have me for the night?"

The old man does not utter a word. Instead, he holds my hand and walks me to the dining room. He serves me some soup and bread. The soup tastes very good. I so much enjoy it, and so does my heart. We try to finish it as fast as possible so as not to keep the old man waiting. He waits for me then leads me to a place where I can shower and get changed. He hands me some clean clothes and closes the door behind me. In the shower I let the warm water run over me and erase any trouble this journey might have caused. I close my eyes and imagine the faces I am going to see at the hospital. I think of all the people I left behind. I miss them all. And I love them all, but I have to do this.

What would I do in a hospital? Would I be of any use? What are their expectations of me? I do not know.

I finish showering, get dressed and step outside to find the old man waiting for me. Again, he is quiet. And I do not wish to disturb his silence. I just follow his steps. He leads me to the room where I would be able to spend the night.

"Get some rest. You will tell me about your journey tomorrow," he says. Then he closes the door behind me and walks away. I feel comfortable and safe in this place. It does not take me a long time to fall asleep. I kiss my heart good night and go deep into a world of dreams. The dreams are vague, but colorful. They make a collage. In this collage, I see pictures of many people I know, some are smiling, some are not. I see a few people crying, but I do not know why. The pictures do not talk. I get scared.

Chapter 5

With The Soldiers

I am not able to communicate with the pictures. Suddenly a voice says, "These are pictures of real people. Try to remember each and every one you see. Each of them has something to say; only you are too far away to hear it." I wake up with this last word in my head to realize that it is still dark outside.

I decide to get up and take a walk. I let my heart sleep. I will go alone this time. While walking I see that some rooms are lit, and others are not. I visit the rooms that are lit. They have wounded soldiers inside. They seem to be in pain. I get inspired to visit the soldiers one at a time. I want to listen to their stories of war, defeat, victory, disappointment, peace and love.

I am not sure where to start. There are several wounded soldiers around me, and each seems to have a different story to tell. I want to listen to all of them. Perhaps I will hear a story which resembles mine. I walk towards one of the soldiers and take a seat next to him. I ask him about how he is doing.

"Those were hard days," he says.

With The Soldiers

"Days of war?" I ask.

"Freedom does not just happen; a lot needs to be sacrificed," he continues. I do not say anything. I remain quiet and give him a chance to proceed.

"We were five friends. We were all drafted at the same time. We were so excited, thinking that war is always a place of victory. We did not think about what might be lost during our journey. Three of my friends had left their wives and children behind. They waited for letters from their families impatiently. Once a month they receive letters. At first, we were winning the war. We did not think of what might happen next. Gradually, things started to get complicated, and we lost the war. Three of my friends did not survive. Two of them had wives and children waiting for them. I was left with only one friend. He was moved to another hospital for treatment. I went through periods of depression. At first, I did not know how to talk to their families. It was one of the hardest times of my life. Then I collected some of their belongings and sent them off with letters of condolences to the families. That was the best decision I ever made."

The soldier stops talking and starts to cry. I wipe his tears with my hands and sit there trying to analyze what he just said. There is not much that can be said. I wipe his tears with my hands again and ask him to get some rest. It is painful, the life of a soldier. It is full of sacrifice and giving.

I get up, take a small walk among the patients, then head to my room. I enter my room so quietly, so as not to wake up my heart. My heart looks so peaceful while sleeping. It appears to be in a different world. I start imagining where it could be now. It may be dreaming. I lie down and decide to sleep too. I need to be ready for the next day. I need to ask and answer questions. I need to know why people come to hospitals, why they go to wars, why some of them make it and others do not. It sure is a world of contradiction.

In the morning, I am awakened by the old man's soft voice. He seems to be talking to the patients, because he is talking in a very low tone. He does not wish to disturb them. I cannot understand what he is saying. He must be a very considerate man. I decide to get up, get dressed and go outside. I walk towards the voice that I hear. I see the old man sitting by one of the patient's bedside. He is saying a prayer. The patient's eyes are closed, and there are signs of peace on his face. I choose not to disturb them. Instead, I stand in silence and wait for the ritual to be completed. When the old man gets done with his prayers, he notices me.

He smiles, utters a few words to the patient then walks towards me.

"Let us go to a quiet place where we can talk," he says.

I follow him in complete trust and silence.

"Did you have a good sleep?" he asks.

"Very good, thank you," I reply.

"What brings you, our way?" he asks kindly.

At this point I do not know what to say. As if I suddenly forgot what had brought me towards the hospital. I suddenly remember my heart. After the conversation is over, I will go and check on it.

"It is a long story," I explain to the old man how I would be glad to tell him my story, if he had the time to hear it.

"If none of the patients need me today, I can be with you as much as possible and hear all about it," he says.

It takes me a while to remember the steps of my journey and how it all started. Then suddenly my heart appears and whispers words of love in my ears. I start remembering the man I love, and a tear slowly falls down my face. I start remembering how we first met, the passion I felt the day I saw him, the medicine he gave me to save my life, and the times of solitude I spent when he was not near.

The old man hands me a napkin to wipe my tears. I start to regain my

With The Soldiers

memory gradually. I go back to the first day when I saw my love; when the whole world stopped, and I could no longer make sense of time and space. I try to explain to the old man how it felt, so he will not be surprised about how I ended up here at the hospital. I tell him about my sister's death and the hardship I had to go through after she died. I tell him about how my beloved healed me with a combination of support and medication. I speak about my transformation and the day I felt I was growing up. The old man is listening patiently, so focused on what I am saying.

I chose not to tell him that I have not spent enough time with my beloved. I just tell him about the love we shared and the joy we brought into each other's lives. The old man puts a smile on his face when I speak about the warmth of the relationship. The smile is so genuine I do not wish to disturb him. But I must when I start telling him about my beloved's disappearance. I tell him about how sudden it was, and how it left me so perplexed, so unable to go on. The old man keeps listening, without making any attempt to interrupt me, as if he knows what happened and what was about to happen. But even with that, the enthusiasm keeps showing on his face and I proceed.

I tell him how the journey started. I do not mention my heart. I do not think the old man will understand. I tell him about the different stages of my journey, the times I got so excited and the times I lost hope, the times I felt warm and protected, and the times it was so cold I almost gave up.

With this, my conversation comes to an end. I do not know what to say next. But I ask the old man if I could stay for a while and help at the hospital. Before he answers me on this, he asks me to be patient regarding the story I just told him. He says that love requires patience and perseverance. That's all he says. Then he tells me that I can stay and help.

I am so happy to hear that, because being among the patients would distract me from thinking too much about my beloved. There are not many people helping out at the hospital, so my presence is important at this point. The old man asks me where I am headed next. To this I have no answer.

Do I really know where I am going? My whole trip has been nothing but an accident. I have let destiny lead me instead of making the choices myself. I have let nature surprise me with its unusual twists and turns. I have allowed my heart to take the lead. How can I tell the old man about my heart? It may sound strange or unreal, so I decide not to tell him after all.

I am ready to volunteer at the hospital. I have had enough wounds to help understand those of others. I have gained some empathy, which would make me fit for the job I am about to start.

I run straight to my room to tell my heart what has just happened. I am so excited. Finally, I am stable somewhere. I now have a place to lay my head and think without interruption; prepare for the next step and dream.

I tell my heart the news, and my heart is happy too. We dance and cheer. My heart tells me to be patient because this is what this kind of job requires. And I promise my heart that I will be.

"And what will you do while I am at work?" I ask.

"I will be beating from far away to remind you that your mission is not yet complete. I will be watching over you, making sure you do not deviate from your purpose. And at the end of the day, I will be here to hear your stories and complaints of the day."

I love what my heart says. My heart cares for me. We are inseparable and essential to the existence of each other. It feels so rewarding at the end of the day to know that my heart will be here, waiting to hear my stories. I am sure my heart will also have stories to tell me; lots of them.

Chapter 6

Stories

Each morning my heart wakes me up to get ready for the day. I wake up and make myself a humble breakfast. I love eating oats, and at the hospital there are lots of them. There are also fruit trees in the backyard. I pick up a few raspberries and mix them with my oats. It is a delicious breakfast.

Each morning, I make sure the patients are getting a breakfast as healthy as mine. I visit the kitchen, speak with the cook and serve the breakfast myself to as many patients as I can. I enjoy feeding them breakfast myself. During that time, they tell me so much about themselves, their stories of war, their achievements and losses, and so on. And I love listening to them.

One wounded soldier tells me about how he got wounded and why he chose to be involved in the war in the first place. Another soldier tells me about the love he had to leave behind when going to war. He tells me his beloved's name is April and that she has hazel eyes. He tells me the stories about each time they met. Each story is different and has a different feel to it. April is two years younger than him, but a lot wiser is what he says. He cannot make a decision without consulting with her first. He tells me how much he is missing her. The last time he had heard from her was a few months back. He has written letters, but they keep coming back. He still writes her letters he said. He wants to keep them until he meets with her. The letters are his way of showing that his love for her has never stopped.

He asks me if we could write her a letter together. And I agree. We sit down, side by side, writing the letter. He tells me what he wants to say, and I write the words. This man loves this woman so dearly. While he is speaking, he starts to cry. And I cannot say a word. All I can do is remember my own love. I remember how many days it has been since I last saw him. I miss him. But it seems that I am stuck right where I am now. I cannot move forward. I must accomplish something. I need to support those who need me. My love for him will not decrease that way. It will only grow stronger. Perhaps by helping others and hearing their stories I will be more motivated to move forward and persevere.

The days are long. But the stories I hear from the patients seem very short, because I enjoy them so much. They are full of adventure, love, harmony and excitement. I get so excited and cannot wait to go back to my room and tell my heart all about it.

Every night my heart is waiting for me impatiently. He warmly welcomes me home, waits till I have rested, then starts asking me about my stories of the day. They are endless. They produce all kinds of feelings in me. I do not know whether I should be hopeful or discouraged after hearing them. Some patients are still in touch with the ones they love. Others are not. I believe both, but I feel sorry for both. None of them can see or feel the ones they love. Just like me, they are full of longing for something they once had, something that had once made them so happy and fulfilled.

How can I explain all that to my heart? Perhaps I do not need to explain. My heart may already feel what I am trying to say. That is the beauty of it. But I still want to talk to my heart, because I enjoy the conversation that goes on between us.

"Do these lovers ever give up?" I ask my heart.

"Lovers do not give up." my heart calmly answers.

I stay up every night, telling my heart about the stories that I hear. Some are happy. Some are very sad. My heart gives me all kinds of feedback, which makes me understand the stories and myself better. My heart is so wise. It can tell me how the stories will end, even before I am finished telling it.

My heart amazes me. It never gets tired of listening. It keeps beating its usual beats. Only when I speak about my own love story does it beat faster than usual. My heart misses listening to my love story. Mine is too complicated; too unpredictable. I want someone to listen; someone who is true and wise. My heart is patient and caring. All I must do is gather my thoughts and start somewhere. I have been keeping my feelings inside since we reached the hospital. And my heart would have asked me, but it wants me to speak naturally, at my own pace. Then I will be speaking the truth of my feelings.

My heart is right. The truth comes out when I feel I am not being pushed to speak it. When we know someone is genuinely listening, we say what we truly feel. And my heart makes me feel it is enjoying the stories I am saying. Here I find myself all over again remembering my one and only love. I have left him somewhere in time. We have been apart for a while now, a while long enough to make me grow older, less enthusiastic and less amused about what goes on around me.

The volunteer work has given me a sense of duty. I feel productive and needed. It is a beautiful feeling. But somehow my feelings are not complete. Something major is missing. My heart knows exactly what I am talking about. Our departure was very peaceful. It was not even a departure, because we did not know it would be the last time we would see each other.

"What happens to lovers when they are no longer there?" I ask my heart.

"Sometimes they try to find a new love, just to forget the one they no longer have. And there are times when they just wait to be found," my heart replies.

"What is this land they hide in?" I ask.

"It is the land of love, a land where mystery is indispensable. Only those who understand that love requires patience and sacrifice can be there."

I agree with my heart. Love sure requires patience. And we never know how capable we are of it until we are faced with a situation that requires it.

It has been a long time since I have seen my love. But I do not give up. I am still hopeful. With the help of my heart, I persevere slowly. I dream about my love and see him in different forms. One time I dreamt him dead. How do I know if he is dead or alive? Dreams do tell us something.

A few nights back I dreamt about my love. He was walking in a forest, and I was watching him from far away. He was collecting wildflowers. When he saw me, he gave me the flowers. But the flowers had thorns that made my hands bleed. He kissed my hands and suddenly disappeared. I wonder about the meaning of this dream. My heart tells me that the thorns represent the pain that I am going through. My heart stops at this point. I do not know if he knows more but does not wish to tell me. I ask no more questions but think of the dream often.

Dreaming about my love is not an unusual thing for me. It often happens. But sometimes I cannot remember the dream. The dreams I have give me a feeling of satisfaction. I feel as if my love and I are connected in the spiritual world. Dreams hold messages, which I am supposed to know. I will know them when the time is right. My heart seems to agree.

I am stuck in time. I can neither proceed, nor go back. I am waiting for a miracle to happen. Each day when I meet with the wounded soldiers, I realize how precious life and love are. I do not wish to waste my time on something less valuable than love. For this I spend as much time possible with the soldiers. Their stories teach me important lessons. Some stories are so bitter. I cannot listen to them without breaking into tears. I had often heard stories from grandmother. But they were all fiction. Despite this fact, I often cried. Now the stories are real, told by people who lived them. That would influence any soul hearing them. I am glad to be part of that. It is a great feeling to witness the joy and misery of real people.

In this I am not alone. My heart is a witness to my stories and that of the soldiers. I am not sure which are more complicated. They both have a theme of love. That's what makes my heart eager to listen. The hospital is always quiet. The only noise one can hear is that of a hurting soldier. Many soldiers are in physical pain. Some are emotionally suffering. And there are others who must deal with both kinds of pain. These are the soldiers I love spending the most time with. I relate to them. We seem to be sharing the same intensity of feelings.

The soldiers often ask me questions. They ask me about the meaning of love, whether I believe they will re-unite with their loved ones, or whether they will survive or not. All those were very hard questions. If only I had the right answers for them. I try to be as positive as possible while answering the questions. That seems to cheer the soldiers' spirits. They need hope, and someone to promise them a better tomorrow. And I am the person to do it.

I am glad to be in such a position. Giving them hope assures me that hope does exist. My heart confirms that so many times hopelessness begets meaningless. Without hope we lose the effort to go on. Hope is important indeed, especially if it is the only thing you have left. You hold on to it tight, afraid of letting go.

It seems there are so many things in life that I cannot let go of. I only knew my beloved for a short while, and I cannot seem to let go of that love. I do not think it matters how long we have known each other. The quality of time we spent was heavenly. We connected on a spiritual level. We read the scriptures together and analyzed what each different book meant.

I cannot imagine for a second that something would separate us.

It must have been against his will. He must be stuck somewhere, unable to tell me where he is or what he has become. In the meantime, while I wait for him, I want to become a better person myself. I want him to be proud of me, even while he's away. Somehow, he may be able to feel the change I am going through. We are connected through our heavenly souls. We may be able to know what is going on with each other, without being together.

I imagine too many things these days. Some are good, some are bad. And your spirit follows me everywhere I go. I never imagined something so invisible to have such a clear presence in my life. Where is my home? Or am I looking for one? I know I lived in your heart once. I did not wish for any other place then. It was so comfortable, so welcoming. Your heart and mine are so alike in that sense. They are both warm. They resemble each other.

I miss your heart. It was so tender, and that reflected in your eyes. It is impossible to forget your eyes. They spoke to me loudly and in silence. They told me stories, without uttering a word. They made me climb the stairs of life with no fear. I truly became fearless. You watched me and smiled. You always told me how proud you were of me. That gave me so much satisfaction. You made me aware of abilities I did not know I had.

You always made me feel good about myself. You must be alive. Our mission on earth is not yet complete. Remember our dreams about leaving the world a better place? What happened to that? You yourself have achieved that dream. You have left me a better person. I can feel it. I am doing it. I am helping soldiers heal. And that feels so good. It is rewarding at the end of the day to know that someone's pain has been eased, only because you listened and gave them some attention. Perhaps that is not much, but to someone who has little hope left, it is a lot.

Chapter 7

Purple Spirit

Tomorrow seems so far away, not only to the soldiers, but also to me. I am not sure how close I am to my destiny. I am not going after my destiny.

I am walking in the path of the unknown, waiting for my destiny to unfold. My heart has been with me on this. We are united towards the same aim. And that seems assuring. What is the possibility that my heart could be wrong? Not a true heart like mine. I believe in my heart the same way I believe in you.

You asked me once to never doubt you. And I have not. I just wonder a lot about what has become of you. How many things happen to us in our lives only to make us more confused, less certain of who we are or what we are capable of becoming? Missing you has done that to me. I am not sure if this is a negative or a positive thing. My journey is not yet over, so I cannot decide. But I know for sure I am confused right now. Without my heart, I probably would gather my things and go back home. I will go and wait with the others who are waiting. I will probably lose hope one day and accept the fact that you exist no more. I

will have a new beginning. Or maybe I will give up on the idea of love completely.

I keep communicating with the soldiers in a language I think they might understand. I try my best to never let them lose hope. I read them the letters they receive. And when there were none, I read them stories of love, which gives them hope as well. My heart is my inspiration. I speak with my heart, and that encourages me to plant hope in the hearts of those who need it most. There are several soldiers who have already healed and gone home. That makes me so joyful. I want all of them to survive, to go back to their loved ones and tell their stories of war, survival and patience.

Patience is a lesson that can be learned from such experiences. One tends to wait for a wound to heal, for a letter to arrive, for a friend to come back and so on. I tend to learn patience, along with the soldiers. Their stories become mine. I do not tell them much about myself. I only share with them my experience of losing my twin sister. They also know that I have a loved one. But the details I keep to myself. I did not mean to, but I do not wish to add complication to their lives. I want to share with them cheerful experiences. I want to tell them about love and the transformation it does to a human soul. I want them to know that no matter how hard we try to forget a loved one, the deeper the love becomes rooted in our hearts.

There is so much I want to share with the soldiers. But the truth is I do not know what my limits are. I do not know what could cause them more pain. Perhaps they wish to forget their loved ones. For this and some other reasons, I decide to stay silent many times. I prefer to listen. And when they ask for my opinion, I give it from a lover's point of view. I always ask them to stay hopeful. I am.

There are new soldiers coming to the hospital every day. And a few volunteers are coming in too. We need more help, but the hospital is far, and not many people know it exists. I often must work extra hours. That does not displease me. I have a place to stay and food to eat. I even make a few friends. And at times when I lose hope, I pray, and then consult either with my heart or the old man. The old man does not know details about my love life. I am scared to speak about it. I do not want to spoil what the future may hold. The old man is very wise and supportive. He knows what I have in mind, even without me having to speak about it.

They say love signs cannot be hidden. They show in the eyes of the lover. People drastically transform when they are in love. Love changes everything, not only the person who is experiencing it. It makes the world a better place. People become more tolerant with love. It is said that love endures all things. And this is what has been happening to me, I have become tolerant of things I never imagined I would experience before. Soldiers were dying in front of my own eyes. The sad part is that those soldiers were hopeful that they were going to get well and reunite with their loved ones. I try to give them a glance of hope. Now I feel that I have betrayed them somehow. I did not mean to do that. I was truly hopeful that they were going to get better and go home.

Days and nights go by, and I am busy taking care of soldiers. I do not have time to have a meaningful conversation with my heart. I do not abandon it. I only know deep inside that my heart understands. I miss talking to it. I am going to make some free time tonight and have a long chat with it. Perhaps my heart has something to tell me.

I am with the soldiers, working as hard and fast as I can. I am dreaming about you. We are somewhere, far away. You are holding my hand, and I am dancing to the rhythm of my own heart. You whisper words in my ear. They make me cheerful. You look the same since I last saw you, only you are more tender. Your eyes carry endless stories in them. I daydream about you each day, and each day you tell me a different story.

I am suddenly awakened by a soldier's cry of pain. A soldier has just arrived. It looks like he is deeply wounded. I run towards him. I see the wound is very deep. I get help, then get close to him and hold his hand. As I hold his hand, I remember how you used to ease my pain by holding my hand. You were with me the times I needed you the most. It was the time when my twin sister died. You were so supportive, so compassionate. I shall never forget that. And I will never forget the medicine you gave me and how well it worked on my sorrow. Is someone taking care of you right where you are? Could you possibly be in pain? I tend to think about pain a lot these days, because I see a lot of suffering around me.

It breaks my heart when a soldier does not recover. If you were here, I would talk to you about it. Perhaps you would have prescribed your natural medications to the soldiers. I am sure that it would help them the same way it helped me.

The day is almost done. A few more hours and I will be back in my room, talking to my heart, telling it about the sweetness and hardship of the day. The days do have sweetness. Every time a soldier recovers, I feel cheerful. It gives me hope about other things in life. It reminds me that things do change, many times for the better. I want to believe this. I want to believe in the good things in life and to keep the faith, the faith that my prayers shall be answered one day.

I pray a lot, and even though I do not get an instant answer, I have a feeling that one day I will.

After completing my duties, I go straight to my room, where my heart lies waiting for me. I feel comfortable just walking into the room. The feeling that someone has been waiting for me gives me so much satisfaction. My heart has been feeling hopeful today. It has told me that. We talk about different aspects of life. I listen and it listens. Some of our ideas are the same, which makes me feel that I am going in the right direction.

We have been in the hospital too long. I have lost count of the days we have spent here. I want to continue with my journey, but something about the wounded soldiers keeps me attached to this place. Their need for my help seems to grow larger. And there are only a few people available at the hospital to help. I seem to belong to this place. Although I have never worked in a hospital before, the job suited me well, because I needed the soldiers as much as they needed me. I needed them and they gave me a home. They needed me and I gave them comfort.

My heart seems to agree as well. It has nothing but words of encouragement for me tonight. We both go to sleep early. During my sleep I have dreams about you. They are not so clear. I keep waking up.

Where do we go when we sleep? Do we ever get to meet the people we dream about? It is a very mysterious world, the world of dreams. It seems so real sometimes one can hardly distinguish it from reality. Or perhaps it is a reality of the spiritual world. Sometimes my dreams are so beautiful I do not wish to wake up. But against my will I am awakened the next morning by the old man's voice, making the procedures of the new soldiers who have just arrived.

It was hard for me to wake up this morning, because I did not sleep well the night before. But knowing that new soldiers have arrived gives me much enthusiasm. I get out of bed, get ready and walk towards the old man.

This is not a dream. I open and close my eyes several times to make sure it is not. Time has frozen for the second time in my life. And all I can see is a face I recognized from a long time ago and a wounded body. It is a face I have been so thirsty to see. I do not know what to do. I do not move or say anything. I want to make sure first that what I am experiencing is real. Perhaps the wounds are the best indication to the reality of the situation. The wounds seem so deep. And so seems your sleep. At this moment I am not sure if you are dead or alive. I look around me.

There are a few other soldiers who are wounded also. And the old man is busy, talking to a staff member. I do not know to whom I should turn. I start walking around the area, like someone who has been hit by a lightning strike. I am crying, yet I am so excited. I need to talk to someone. The old man must know something, but he is too busy now.

This is happening. By the grace of God, it is happening. My prayers have been answered. I take a few steps towards you and touch your face. You open your eyes and shut them right back. You are alive! I want to let the whole world know, but I do not wish to disturb the other patients. You seem to be in pain. I do not know what to do. I am afraid to touch you. I stand still and wait for something to happen. What do I do with myself now that you are here? Where do I hide my tears? I look at you for a very long time. I want you to wake up, recognize me and take me in your arms. But you seem so far away.

The old man asks me to continue with my duties, but I am incapable. How can I explain to the old man what has just happened? I am not able to utter a word. Perhaps I have to run back to my room and tell my heart about it. With my heart I do not need to use many words. I run to my room, only to find my heart smiling and waiting for me.

"Do you know?" I ask.

"Know what?" my heart replies.

"That my beloved is back. He is outside."

"I am not surprised. I had a feeling this would happen."

"Why did you not tell me?"

"I wanted to see how far you were going to go with your journey." "Is he going to make it?" I ask.

"That I do not know," my heart softly replies.

"I need to get back there. Pray for me dear heart of mine."

With those words I leave the room and walk towards my beloved. He is still sleeping. The old man reminds me of the duties I have to complete. I try my best to get started. I finally do, but I am not focused. My heart and my mind are with my beloved.

I spend some time with the soldiers then go back to the old man and ask him about my beloved's condition.

"We still do not know if he will make it or not." he says.

Tears fill my eyes when I hear him say that, and I do not know what to say. The old man notices my tears, but he does not say anything. "Could this really be happening to me?" I was supposed to walk to my destiny. And here it is, walking towards me. Life is strange indeed. We do not know what to expect. Things we expect to happen never occur. And things we never imagined occurring suddenly do happen.

I want someone to explain to me the perplexity of the situation, but there is no one around. I cannot go back to my room. I could talk to my heart, but I cannot leave my duties right at this moment. The hours are going by so slow. I work with the soldiers and check on my beloved every time I have a chance. He is not conscious. Doctors come in and out of the room to check on his condition. I am scared to ask them anything. I do not wish to hear that he is not going to make it. "My dearest, I am waiting for you to wake up. I have longed for this moment for such a long time. Days and nights could not erase the love I have for you. I need you to shine on my life again. Be well and come back soon. I am waiting."

These are the words I whisper into his ears while he sleeps. I do not wish to wake him up, yet how I want him to hear me. I sit down quietly by his side and pray for the Lord of all humankinds to bring him back to me, to help him get well. He is in a deep sleep. Where do we go when we sleep like that? Is this considered a death? I do not know.

I walk towards the radio and play some soft music. This will put his spirit at ease. Music is a universal language of love, peace and hope. I truly believe this. I want him to be surrounded by such positive energy, even if he is unable to hear it. He may still be able to feel it.

I stay up all night watching you. The old man asks me several times to go back to my room, but I tell him that I am not tired. I want to tell him all about this, but somehow the time is not right. I will tell him later.

I go back to my room several times and speak to my heart. My heart asks me to relax and have faith. I try. I ask my heart more questions. It does not reply to all of them, simply because it does not know all the answers. There are always limitations to what any of us creatures is capable of knowing. My heart does not put my hopes too high, or too low. It is being realistic.

I walk back to my beloved's room. He is still asleep. I lay down by his side, hold his hand and close my eyes. His hand starts to move. I do not know what to do. I sit there and wait for another move. His hands are so warm. The warmth extends to my whole body. I still cannot believe that he is here, next to me.

Even though he is asleep, we are still able to connect. I whisper again into his ear, but he does not seem to hear me. I decide to tell him a short story, a story of how much I love him and the destiny that allowed us to collide once more.

While I am reading, my beloved opens his eyes and looks straight into mine. I do not know what is happening to me now. I can hardly catch my breath. I do not utter a word. All I do is smile at him and cry at the same time.

He keeps looking at me. But he is unable to say much. I wonder if he recognizes me. Tears fill his eyes as he reaches for my hand. He holds my hand and again says nothing.

We both cry as we sit there, not sure what to do with the moment. Or maybe we are too sure but are incapable. I sit there facing him, unable to move an inch. I gaze into his eyes again. He seems to be in so much pain.

I wish I could ease it. I wish I could make it go away.

"What brings you here?" he finally says.

"My destiny," I say.

He smiles and proceeds. "How long have you been here?"

"I have lost count of the days."

I suddenly remember that I need to inform the doctor that he is awake. I go get the doctor and remain outside the room while he checks my beloved. I wait outside for a while. After that the doctor walks towards me and tells me that the patient's condition is improving. I go back to the room and see that my beloved is waiting for me. At this moment, now that he is awake, now that he is here, I do not know whether to be happy or mad at him. I spent too many days and nights waiting, not knowing what had happened to him. His spirit was following me around wherever I go. And I could never let go. How could something so invisible have such a clear presence in our lives? I do not know. Now he is here, but suddenly I am unable to ask him all these questions, perhaps because he is injured.

"I want to hear everything," he says.

The truth is I am the one who needs to hear everything. I need some words to calm me down. Only I do not know what questions to ask. I have too many questions in my head.

"Are you still taking your medications?" he asks.

"I am not."

"How come?"

"I got distracted."

"With what?"

"With losing you."

"Was that hard?"

"Very much so."

"Is that what brought you here?"

"Yes, somehow."

"Did you come alone?"

"No! I brought my heart with me." He laughs.

I interrupt him by saying, "For a while I thought I would never see you again."

"That must have been hard." he replied.

"It was."

I want him to tell me about every single detail that has happened to him since I last saw him. I want to tell him everything myself. I want to cry on his shoulder. I want him to know how much I still love him.

That night I tell him about all that I went through. There were small events which I had completely forgotten. I tell him about how hard the nights and days were that I spent without him. I tell him about how I left everything behind and came on with my journey. I tell him about the dreams.

"What made you think you would make it?" he interrupts.

"I had my heart with me all along the way," I say.

"Your heart?"

"Yes! You can speak to it and ask it if you wish. I spoke to it in my darkest moments."

"I believe you. My heart could feel you at times. It told me that."

"Your heart is true."

"And so is yours."

"Tell me about the hardships you went through," he instructs.

"The toughest moments were the ones when I thought I would never see you again," I reply.

"What made you think so?"

"You were gone for a long time. It was so sudden, so unpredictable."

"Isn't life like this too?"

"Yes, sometimes."

"How did you end up here at the hospital?"

"There was a light that I followed. It led me here."

"It must have been the same light that led me here as well."

"It must have been."

That night my love spoke to me about his sudden imprisonment, about the days and nights he wished to be with me, and the hardship he went through.

He was imprisoned for something he did not do.

"Injustice is one of the hardest things that could happen to us," he said.

"I longed for this moment for so long." he continued. "I also thought I would never see you again.

Love is like that. It takes us by complete surprise sometimes. It requires patience and perseverance, as they say. And I learned that no matter how hard the journey, it is sure worth taking.

There is a purpose in why love makes us suffer sometimes. It happens to us to make us question our own existence. Perhaps that needs to be questioned from time to time. This is what leads us to take the journey in the first place. It leads us to self-discovery and evolution. This great thing called love is what makes us better beings, able to help one another.

Simply, it transforms us into something we never imagined we could be.

Milton Keynes UK
Ingram Content Group UK Ltd.
UKHW020906260724
446053UK00007B/20

9 798330 285679